Hidden Treasures of the Past

Adam Ford

Contents

Hidden Treasures

What Are Treasures?

A treasure can be many different things. It can be gold and silver, or jewels. But a treasure can also be a painting, an old book, a crumbling **ruin** or even the remains of a person who lived long ago.

Sometimes, very old objects, ruins or remains are so rare and important that they are described as "treasures of the past".

Mist covers the ancient ruins of Machu Picchu in Peru.

Over hundreds or thousands of years, treasures can become hidden and lost. But how?

Some treasures are buried and then forgotten. Others are destroyed by a natural disaster, or slowly fall down over the years and disappear under plants and leaves, then under soil.

Then, one day, someone stumbles on a crumbling old wall in a forest, or an **archaeologist** digs a hole, and treasures that have lain hidden are found again.

The Terracotta Warriors were buried under the ground in China for over 2000 years.

The Golden Mask of Tutankhamen

The golden mask of Tutankhamen (say: *Too-tan-ka-men*) is one of the most famous ancient treasures ever discovered. Tutankhamen was a **pharaoh** (say: *fair-oh*), or king, who ruled Egypt over 3000 years ago. The pharaohs were rich and powerful, and the Egyptian people believed them to be gods. Tutankhamen was one of the richest and most powerful pharaohs of them all.

The mask of Tutankhamen weighs over 10 kilograms.

This wall painting from ancient Egypt shows Tutankhamen and some gods.

Tutankhamen was buried wearing this golden mask.

Ancient Egyptians believed that after a person died, they went on to live another life. They called this the "afterlife". Often, the dead were buried in **tombs** with objects they would need in the afterlife, including food, clothes and weapons. Their bodies were also prepared for the next life. They were **preserved** by a process called "mummification". The mummies of the pharaohs were buried in golden coffins, along with many other treasures. A pharaoh's coffin is called a "sarcophagus" (say: *sar-kof-a-guss*).

Many Egyptian tombs were broken into and the treasures stolen by robbers thousands of years ago. But the tomb of Tutankhamen remained hidden in a place called the Valley of the Kings until it was discovered by the English archaeologist Howard Carter in 1922.

The tomb of Tutankhamen is in the Valley of the Kings in Egypt.

Tutankhamen was buried with many **precious** objects including jewellery, weapons, statues, furniture and even **chariots** made of gold. One of the greatest treasures found inside the tomb was the golden mask of Tutankhamen. It is made of gold and jewels and is thought to show the face of Osiris (say: *Oh-sy-ris*), the god of the afterlife.

The inside of the tomb of Tutankhamen was crowded with treasures.

The City of Pompeii

Pompeii (say: *Pom-pay*) was a busy Roman city on the Italian coast of the Mediterranean Sea. Thousands of years ago, in 79 **CE**, the city was destroyed by the violent volcanic eruption of nearby Mount Vesuvius.

On an autumn morning almost 2000 years ago, the people of Pompeii were going about their daily lives. Children walked to school; their parents shopped or worked. On the seashore, fishermen unloaded their catches. In the beautiful and richly decorated houses, **enslaved** workers tended the gardens and prepared meals.

In the distance, smoke rose from Mount Vesuvius. The people of Pompeii were used to seeing smoke, but on that day, the volcano exploded with terrible force. The ground shook, causing buildings in Pompeii to collapse.

From the top of the mountain gushed a huge cloud of hot ash and poisonous gas that flowed down its sides. The deadly cloud burnt olive groves and **vineyards**, and buried the city of Pompeii.

Some of the people escaped in boats, but the eruption happened so quickly that many died in their homes and workplaces, and were buried under a thick layer of grey ash. Within a few days, the city of Pompeii had completely disappeared.

Mount Vesuvius can be seen behind the ruins of Pompeii.

Some of the grand buildings in Pompeii were already hundreds of years old when they were buried.

Beneath the ash, the well-preserved remains of the city lay hidden and forgotten until archaeologists discovered them many hundreds of years later.

Beautiful paintings on the walls of the houses show how the Roman people dressed. The ruins of the **temples** tell us what gods they prayed to. Seeds and animal bones found in the ash show what they ate.

From the ruins of Pompeii, archaeologists were able to piece together stories of the people who lived 2000 years ago, and show that treasure does not have to be made of gold.

This is one of the paintings found in the ruins of Pompeii.

The Ruins of Machu Picchu

High in the Andes Mountains in Peru, South America, lies Machu Picchu (say: *Ma-choo Pee-choo*), the most famous ruin of the ancient Inca people. The Inca people lived and worked on the steep mountainsides and deep valleys over 500 years ago. Their **empire** was large and powerful. Their lands stretched along the Andes Mountains for thousands of kilometres.

Most Inca people lived a simple life, farming the valleys and lower slopes of the mountains. They grew fruits and vegetables and kept herds of llamas and alpacas.

One of the first great Incan kings, Pachacuti (say: *Pa-cha-koo-ti*), built a palace on a narrow ridge in the mountains, high above the Urubamba River Valley. The palace was used by Incan kings for almost a hundred years, between 1438 and 1533.

This statue of King Pachacuti was put up in the city of Cusco, Peru, in 1991.

The ruins of Machu Picchu are high in the Andes Mountains.

Today, the remains of the Incan palace are called Machu Picchu. They are enormous ruins of over 200 buildings that include a royal palace, a temple, royal tombs, and houses for hundreds of servants.

The Inca people believed that architecture (the design of buildings) was a kind of art. The buildings at Machu Picchu show the best of Incan architecture. They are made from huge rocks. With great skill, each rock has been carefully carved and polished to fit together perfectly.

The buildings of Machu Picchu were made from huge carved rocks.

In 1533, the Inca people left Machu Picchu forever. The reasons are not clear. Over time, the buildings disappeared from view, buried by the rainforest. The palace was mostly forgotten, remembered only in the stories of the local people. Machu Picchu was rediscovered by the American explorer Hiram Bingham in 1911.

The ruins show the great artistic skills of the Inca people. Built high on a mountain ridge surrounded by rainforest, Machu Picchu is one of the most incredible archaeological treasures in the world.

The ruins of Machu Picchu are often covered in mist.

The Terracotta Warriors

In 1974, some farmers were digging a **well** in the Chinese countryside. As they dug into the ground, they uncovered a life-sized statue of a **warrior**. Following this discovery, archaeologists found a huge army of more than 8000 warrior statues, buried under the surrounding fields. The statues had been buried in lines, as if ready for battle.

The warrior statues are made of terracotta, which is a type of pottery. Archaeologists believe they were made over 2000 years ago, to watch over the tomb of the first **emperor** of China, Qin Shi Huang (say: *Chin Shi Hwang*).

Two thousand years ago, Emperor Qin Shi Huang would have needed thousands of very skilled craftspeople working over many years to make the warriors. Even today, it is very difficult to make pottery sculptures of this size. No two statues in the "Terracotta Army" are the same. Each one has a different face, they are of different heights and they would have all been painted in bright colours.

Before they were buried, the statues would have been colourfully painted.

The Terracotta Warriors and the emperor's tomb were built while Qin Shi Huang was alive. When the emperor died, his tomb and the army of warriors were buried. Over many years, both the emperor's tomb and his army of statues were forgotten.

While most of the army has now been uncovered, the tomb of Emperor Qin Shi Huang has not yet been **excavated**, and it is believed that many more treasures may be hidden inside.

The Terracotta Warrior statues have stood in rows for over 2000 years.

This painting was uncovered in the ruins of Pompeii.

A treasure can be an object made of gold and jewels, like the mask of Tutankhamen. But crumbling old ruins, dusty wall paintings and buried statues can also be treasures because, when they are finally uncovered, they can tell us important stories about people of the past.

Howard Carter's Field Diary

Sunday, 26 November 1922

Yesterday, after years of digging through the desert sands, I found it! At first, it looked like just a plain stone slab in the dirt. But as we dug further, we found that it was the top of a flight of steps, leading down into the base of the hillside. It was the entrance to a tomb!

But not just any tomb. Carved on the sealed door of the tomb was Tutankhamen's royal symbol. With growing excitement, we broke open the door. Stale air rolled out of the darkness. With shaking hands, I shone a torch into the gloom. My friend Lord Carnarvon said, "Can you see anything?" I replied, "Yes, wonderful things."

The tomb was stacked with hundreds of objects. Gold and jewels glittered in the torchlight.

the entrance to Tutankhamen's tomb

This photo shows the treasures we found piled up in the tomb.

Wednesday, 29 November 1922

After days of searching the tomb, we had not found Tutankhamen's mummy. Where could it be? We were just about to give up when I spied another blocked-up doorway, behind a pile of golden furniture. I crawled under a royal bed and broke through the doorway to see a space just large enough for me to crawl through. Choking dust made me cough, but I pushed forward and swept my torchlight into the darkness.

Suddenly, the room glowed as the light bounced off a golden sarcophagus. At last, after 3000 years, the young pharaoh was found.

Carefully, we lifted the heavy lid from the sarcophagus. I gasped. The most beautiful golden mask stared back at me and I knew that I had found the greatest treasure in all of Egypt – and maybe the world.

This photo shows me examining the sarcophagus with the help of an assistant.

Glossary

archaeologist (*noun*) a person who studies very old objects and ruins to understand history

CE (*noun*) Common Era, the time that dates are counted from

chariots (*noun*) vehicles with two wheels, pulled by horses

emperor (*noun*) the ruler of an empire

empire (*noun*) a group of countries with a single ruler

enslaved (*verb*) forced to work without pay, and not allowed to leave

excavated (*verb*) dug out of the ground

pharaoh (*noun*) a ruler in ancient Egypt

precious (*adjective*) valuable and important

preserved (*verb*) kept in good condition

ruin (*noun*) an old building that is partly destroyed

temples (*noun*) buildings for praying to gods

tombs (*noun*)	rooms, usually underground, for burying the dead
vineyards (*noun*)	fields where grapes are grown
warrior (*noun*)	a soldier or fighter
well (*noun*)	a hole dug in the ground to reach water

Index